Beyond the Gray

A Journey of Overcoming and Belonging

Scott W Possley

Imperfection Wellness

Library of Congress Cataloging-in-Publication Data
Possley, Scott William.
Beyond the Gray / by Scott William Possley.
Paperback ISBN: 979-8-9911786-3-1
eBook ISBN: 979-8-9911786-4-8

Young adult fiction
Coming-of-age—Fiction
Self-discovery—Fiction
Mental health—Fiction

Library of Congress Control Number: 2025900176
First printing, February 2025

Cover design by João Cabral

Preface

This is a work of self-help fiction. It was created with the support of AI to tell a story in support of using a framework to get unstuck from negative, ruminating thoughts, thought patterns and self-beliefs. I always felt like I was my thoughts and beliefs and what they said about me. I was associated as one with and believed these negative thoughts and self-beliefs. This often took me to a dark place, and I didn't know where to turn.

It wasn't until 2023 when I had my own personal awakening and I was inspired to take ten universal truths and put them into nine pillars and call it Possley's Paradigm. The paradigm is a free roadmap and mental health resource for all of us who may be suffering. More information can be found in the "Additional Resources" section at the end of this book.

Please enjoy this book for what it is, a story to help support finding and using a paradigm to set us free from the never-ending mental chatter, so that we may find contentment in the here and now—the present moment. And if you take nothing else from this book, just know this: ***You are separate from what your thoughts say about you and the world around you!*** This is yet another universal truth and it is the most important thing I have learned over the years that I share with you today. This paradigm transformed my life. The good days are now great, and the bad days can be tough, but now I have hope, a roadmap and a plan for when I get stuck, and I wish that for you as well.

*"One of the greatest atrocities
to affect humankind
is that we believe
what our thoughts
say about us and
the world around us."*

~Scott W. Possley

Contents

Chapter One

Sam's laughter was like sunlight spilling through the window—warm, inviting, and contagious. They lived in a small, vibrant town where everyone knew each other, and every day felt like an adventure. Sam was the kind of child who radiated joy, with a constant sparkle in their eyes and a boundless energy that seemed to lift the spirits of everyone around them.

Their days were spent with friends, their time split between impromptu games of tag, skipping stones by the creek, and gathering in the park to share stories. Sam's friends loved their sense of humor, their ability to find beauty in the simplest things, and the way they could make anyone feel like they belonged.

On weekends, Sam's parents would take them on nature walks, through fields dotted with wildflowers, and down winding trails where the scent of pine filled the air. Sam would run ahead, stopping only to pick a handful of daisies, or to inspect an ant trail as if it held the secrets of the universe. There was an ease to their happiness, a quiet confidence in the way they embraced the world around them. Sam had never known anything but love, acceptance, and joy.

They were surrounded by a community that encouraged them to be themselves, to speak their mind, and to share their heart. It was the kind of childhood that people spoke about in nostalgic tones—one of pure, untainted happiness, where every moment seemed golden.

Sam was the sun in a sky that always seemed to shine. Their laugh, bright and unrestrained, was a constant melody that danced through the halls of their home and spilled out onto the sidewalks of the neighborhood. The house was cozy, filled with the scent of warm cookies on rainy afternoons and the soft hum of music playing in the background. Sam's parents, warm-hearted and endlessly supportive, fostered a love of imagination in everything they did.

At night, the family would gather in the living room, where the flickering light of a crackling fire cast playful shadows on the walls. Sam's mom would read them stories, her voice soft and comforting, and their dad would play guitar, letting the music weave around the stories as they all settled into a space of deep, shared contentment. There was always a sense of togetherness—an unspoken understanding that nothing in the world was more important than the bond they shared.

Sam, for all their energy, had a particular love for the stars. After dinner, they would often drag their parents out into the backyard, pulling blankets and pillows, and spreading them out on the cool grass beneath the vast night sky. Sam would lie there, gazing up in awe, asking endless questions about constellations, planets, and everything that twinkled overhead. Sometimes, they would imagine the stars as little points of light connecting them to something far beyond, and in those moments, Sam felt infinite.

Sam's friends, who were just as carefree and full of life as they were, were never far behind. There was Anna, who was always up for an adventure, no matter how spontaneous, and Milo, who had an uncanny ability to make everyone laugh, no matter how quiet the day felt. Together, the three of them would spend hours in the park, inventing games, telling stories, and forming a world of their own, where nothing was impossible. They built secret forts in the trees, crafted imaginary kingdoms, and created rituals for every season.

There were no boundaries to their imaginations. Sam would often lead the charge, organizing everyone with an infectious enthusiasm, their voice ringing out in the bright afternoon sun. They weren't just a part of their group—they were its heartbeat, the one who pulled everyone together and reminded them that joy could be found in the smallest of moments.

As the days passed, Sam's world was filled with these small, perfect pieces of happiness—moments of laughter, the softness of the wind through the trees, and the comfort of knowing they were surrounded by love. Every day felt like a gift, and Sam embraced each one with open arms, unaware that their life would soon take an unexpected turn.

But for now, they were the center of their own universe, and nothing seemed more important than the friends they shared, the family they cherished, and the adventures that awaited them at every corner.

Sam's happiness wasn't just about the people around them—it was in the very air they breathed, in the way the world seemed to greet them every morning with open arms. They had a unique way of seeing life through a lens of wonder. Every detail was worth noticing: the soft rustle of leaves in the wind, the way sunlight danced off the surface of the creek, the scent of fresh rain on the earth, or the bright red berries that seemed to appear overnight on the bushes near the garden. Each of these little moments felt like an invitation to pause, to appreciate, to be present. Sam's world was full of magic, woven into the fabric of every day.

Each year, the town would hold a festival downtown, and Sam's eyes would light up like the lights strung up between the trees. There were games, cotton candy, and a big carousel that spun in a circle, filling the air with the sound of joyous music. Sam would always race to the carousel first, eager to climb onto their favorite horse—a white one with a golden mane. They would hold tightly to the painted pole, spinning in dizzying circles, grinning from ear to ear. The day was theirs, every year, and it felt like the whole world belonged to them in those moments.

Sam's friends, too, had become a part of this rhythm. Their friendship was one of those rare, effortless kinds—the kind where time could pass, yet when they reunited, it was as if no time had gone by. When they weren't playing in the park, they would have sleepovers at each other's houses, telling stories well past bedtime, making shadow puppets on the walls, and sharing secrets in the quiet of the night. Sam's laughter would spill into the night air, filling the house with warmth.

Even when the days grew colder, and the first hints of autumn began to settle in, Sam's joy didn't waver. They were the first to suggest making leaf piles in the yard, leaping into them with reckless abandon, their joyful squeals echoing through the crisp air. And when winter arrived with its icy winds and frost-covered windows, Sam would stand at the window, pressing their face against the cool glass, watching the world transform into a glistening wonderland. Snow days were their favorite—days where everything slowed down, and they could spend hours building snowmen, making snow angels, and playing games of hide and seek in the fresh snow.

Their connection with nature was undeniable. Sam would often disappear into the woods behind their house, a place filled with towering trees and hidden paths. They'd walk quietly, taking in the sights and sounds of the forest, pausing to watch squirrels leap from branch to branch or listen to the wind as it rustled through the leaves. The forest, for Sam, was a sanctuary—a place where they could hear the quiet hum of the world's heartbeat and feel a deep, peaceful connection to everything around them.

At night, after long days filled with laughter, adventure, and discovery, Sam would lie in bed, the weight of sleep pulling them under, their mind buzzing with all the stories they would tell the next day. Their family's love surrounded them like a warm blanket, and Sam knew, deep in their heart, that they were safe, that they were enough, and that their world would always be filled with possibilities.

It was a life built on simplicity, but to Sam, it was nothing short of magical. Every smile, every hug, every moment of joy felt like the kind of treasure that would last forever. They didn't yet know that the world wasn't always as kind or as simple as the one they'd built for themselves, but for now, in their bubble of happiness, there was nothing to worry about. Sam was the sun, and the world revolved around them with light and warmth.

Chapter Two

As the years passed, the seasons continued their gentle dance, each one painting Sam's world with new colors and experiences. The small town, with its familiar streets and cozy corners, remained a place where everything felt safe, and Sam was still the heart of it all—loved, cherished, and free to explore the world around them. But time, as it always does, began to move forward, and with it came the inevitable changes that all children must face.

Grade school came to an end, and Sam found themselves standing at the threshold of a new chapter: high school. They'd spent the last few months preparing, excited yet nervous, uncertain of what awaited them in the halls of a much larger school. Gone were the days of small, close-knit classrooms where everyone knew each other by name, and every corner of the school felt like home. High school was bigger, more bustling, and full of unknowns.

The first day of freshman year arrived with the crispness of fall in the air. Sam stood at the bus stop, their backpack slung over one shoulder, feeling a mix of anticipation and unease. The familiar faces of their elementary school friends were scattered around them, but something about the day felt different. They were no longer the playful children they had been just a few months ago. In their place, there was the growing awareness of change—that the world outside of their little bubble was much larger, more complicated.

As the bus pulled away from the curb, Sam sat by the window, watching the landscape blur past. They remembered the simple days of grade school, where everything felt so easy. Now, high school loomed ahead like a vast unknown. It wasn't just the building itself that felt so different—it was the people, the expectations, and the sense of distance that seemed to grow between them and the world they had once known so well.

Sam's friends, Anna and Milo, had gone off to different schools, but Sam had kept in touch with them, their laughter and lightness still a part of their heart. Still, the changes felt more pronounced with each passing day. The days grew longer, the subjects harder, and the cliques of high school, with their unspoken rules and invisible boundaries, seemed more apparent than ever. Sam tried to find their place, to fit into the rhythm of this new chapter, but something felt off. It wasn't that they didn't try—they did, with their usual enthusiasm and warmth. They still smiled brightly in the halls, still made small talk with classmates, but beneath it all, Sam began to feel a sense of disconnection.

The laughter, once so effortless, was now a little quieter. The light-hearted adventures with friends didn't come as easily anymore. Sam felt the pressure to be someone they weren't quite sure they were yet, to conform in ways that felt strange, to hide pieces of themselves to avoid standing out. It wasn't that anyone was unkind, not exactly—but there was a subtle shift in the air, an undercurrent of expectations they hadn't quite anticipated.

Sam tried to cling to the joy that once defined them. They joined clubs, tried to keep the same social energy, but the effort was beginning to drain them. There were more moments of silence between laughter, more questions about what they really wanted, and more uncertainty about who they were supposed to be now.

And yet, they couldn't shake the feeling that something—something deep inside—was starting to shift. The weight of it wasn't heavy yet, just a quiet stirring, like a breeze that brushes your skin before a storm. It was small enough that Sam could ignore it most days, but on some nights, it lingered like a shadow at the edges of their thoughts.

It wasn't just the schoolwork that felt overwhelming—it was the way people seemed to categorize one another so easily. Sam had always prided themselves on their ability to connect with anyone, but high school was different. The ease with which they had once moved through life seemed harder now. There were labels everywhere, groups everywhere, and everyone seemed to fit into their neat little boxes—except for Sam.

They had once known exactly who they were, but as the days passed and the challenges of high school began to unfold, Sam wasn't so sure anymore. They began to wonder if they had been too carefree, too naive. The world outside their happy bubble seemed much more complex, and no matter how hard they tried, they couldn't shake the feeling that something was slipping away, just out of reach.

As the weeks went on, Sam's world began to feel less like the joyful place it once was. The lightness that had always defined them was slowly replaced by a heaviness they couldn't quite explain. At first, it was just a passing thought here and there, a flicker of uncertainty, something Sam could easily push aside. But over time, it grew harder to ignore. It started with the smallest questions, ones Sam would have once brushed off without a second thought.

"What if they don't like me?"
"What if I mess up or fail?"
"Am I really enough as I am?"
"I just don't know what's wrong with me and I just want to be like everyone else!"

It was subtle at first, almost like a passing cloud on an otherwise clear day. Sam would find themselves staring at the mirror, their reflection suddenly unfamiliar, the questions echoing in their mind, tainting their once-confident gaze. It felt like a small, quiet crack forming in their once-perfect world.

But then, the voice grew louder.

It wasn't a voice that Sam recognized—certainly not the voice of their childhood, full of hope and joy. This voice was different. Cold, uninviting. It had a sharp edge to it, like a distant whisper that seemed to come from inside their own head, but from somewhere deep within, like a stranger who had moved in without permission.

It wasn't kind. It wasn't reassuring.

"You're not good enough. You don't belong here. What are you even doing? Everyone else has it together. Why don't you?"

Sam would try to shake it off, force a smile, distract themselves with a quick conversation or a fun activity, but the voice kept returning. It followed them throughout the school day, lingering like a shadow over every interaction, every decision, every moment.

When they walked into the lunchroom, they felt the weight of every pair of eyes on them, even though no one was looking. They imagined people whispering, judging, laughing behind their backs. In the hallways, they couldn't help but second-guess every conversation, wondering if they'd said something wrong, if they'd laughed too loudly, if they'd smiled too wide. Every word they spoke seemed to echo in their mind, and they couldn't shake the feeling that they were constantly on the verge of embarrassing themselves.

At first, Sam didn't know what to call it. They thought it was just normal growing pains—maybe they were just adjusting to a new phase of life. But soon, the doubt became louder, more insistent. It crept into everything. It turned moments of uncertainty into moments of overwhelming fear. And it wasn't just about school. It was about everything.

Sam found themselves lying awake at night, their mind racing with worry, thinking of all the things they had done wrong during the day—things that had seemed insignificant at the time but now felt like monumental failures. The voice would return, reminding them of all their perceived flaws, magnifying every mistake, every misstep, until Sam couldn't tell what was real anymore. Were they really as confident as they had once thought? Or had that been an illusion? Were they just fooling themselves all along?

"I can't do this anymore," Sam whispered to the empty room one night, their chest tight with anxiety. "Maybe I was never meant to be this happy. Maybe I'm just... too much."

The now familiar voice from within was there, waiting.

"Yes, you are too much. You don't fit in. You'll never be good enough for anyone."

Sam tried to shake it off, tried to remind themselves of the person they used to be—the person who could laugh freely, who could love openly, who believed in themselves with all their heart. But no matter how hard they tried, the voice wouldn't stop. It filled their head like a constant hum, always present, always feeding the doubt, feeding the fear.

And the worst part? Sam wasn't sure if they could trust their own thoughts anymore. Had they always been this way? Had they always had these insecurities, buried deep beneath the surface, just waiting for the right moment to rise up? Or had this voice—this constant stream of doubt and worry—only come to life because of the pressure of high school, the unfamiliarity of the new environment, the need to fit in, to be perfect, to be seen?

Sam started to wonder if the voice was them. If the thoughts they were having, the constant self-criticism and second-guessing, was just who they were. They became entangled in the web of their own mind, feeling more and more disconnected from the confident, carefree person they used to be.

The world, once so full of possibility and light, now felt suffocating. Every day felt like a battle between who they used to be and who they thought they were becoming. They wanted so desperately to return to that carefree joy, to that person who believed in themselves without question—but it felt like the more they tried to find their way back, the more the voice tightened its grip.

Over time, Sam found themselves slipping further into the grip of their inner doubts. What had once been fleeting moments of uncertainty now became a constant, pervasive presence. The voice grew louder, more persistent, lurking in the background of their mind, waiting for the right moment to make itself known. It felt like a dark cloud had descended upon them, and no matter how hard they tried to shake it off, it lingered, hanging over every thought, every word, every decision.

At first, Sam tried to resist the voice. They tried to remind themselves of who they were—of the vibrant, confident child who had once walked through life without a second thought about their worth or place in the world. But the more they tried to push the voice away, the stronger it became. It started to invade every part of their life, seeping into their thoughts until they could no longer distinguish between their own mind and the voice that had taken root inside them.

In the mornings, Sam would wake up feeling exhausted, even before the day had started. They used to love mornings—the soft warmth of the sun creeping through the window, the excitement of a new day full of possibilities. But now, as soon as they opened their eyes, the thoughts would begin, racing through their mind like a whirlwind.

"Why are you even trying? You know you'll mess up. They're all going to laugh at you. You're just not good enough anymore."

The weight of these thoughts felt suffocating, as if they were standing in a dense fog, unable to see clearly, unable to move freely. Sam couldn't tell anymore whether they were just thoughts or whether they were actually the truth.

The more they listened, the more they began to believe this inner voice. The voice wasn't some distant entity—it was a part of them. It came from inside their own mind, and if the thoughts were coming from them, then they must be true, right? Sam had always prided themselves on their ability to trust their own instincts, to know themselves deeply. But now, everything was clouded. The confidence they had once had felt like a distant memory, and in its place, there was only doubt. It was as if the very essence of who they were had become tangled with the voice.

Sam started to question everything. Who were they without these thoughts? Were they even the same person they used to be, or had they always been this uncertain, this afraid? If these thoughts were coming from them, then maybe they were just broken. Maybe they were always meant to feel this way—lost, insecure, unworthy.

It was like walking through life with a heavy fog in their mind. No matter where they looked, everything seemed to be shrouded in uncertainty. They couldn't focus on anything without the voice creeping in, questioning their every move. When they looked at their friends, they saw the smiles, the easy conversations, the way everyone else seemed to have it together. And Sam? Sam felt like an imposter, pretending to belong, pretending to be just as confident as everyone else.

The voice followed them everywhere. It was there when they spoke in class, when they laughed with friends, when they sat alone in their room at night. The more they thought about it, the more the lines blurred between who they truly were and who the voice told them they were. It was like the voice had become an extension of their identity—something so deeply ingrained in their mind that they couldn't separate it from themselves anymore.

Sam started to avoid situations that triggered the voice. They stopped volunteering to speak in class, even though they used to love sharing their ideas. They withdrew from group activities, avoiding moments where they might stand out or, worse, be criticized. Every action felt weighed down by the fear that the voice might be right—that they didn't belong, that they weren't good enough.

When they passed by the mirror in the hallway, they no longer saw the same person looking back. The reflection seemed foreign, distant, like someone else entirely. They didn't recognize the person staring at them, unsure and filled with doubt. It felt like that person in the mirror couldn't possibly be the same Sam who used to smile freely, who used to trust in their own worth. No, that person didn't exist anymore.

Instead of being able to embrace their uniqueness, Sam began to shrink away from it. They started believing that the doubts they had, the fears, the insecurities, were not just thoughts—they were their identity. If they didn't believe in themselves anymore, then maybe they weren't worth believing in. They couldn't imagine a world where the voice didn't define them, where they weren't bound by it.

The voice, now a constant companion, filled the silence of their thoughts with cruel certainty: "You don't belong. You will never be good enough to fit in, to be loved, to be accepted."

Sam felt like they were drowning in it, like the more they tried to swim to the surface, the deeper they sank into the darkness. It wasn't just the thoughts anymore—it was everything. It was the belief that the voice wasn't something outside of them. It was a reflection of who they were, a confirmation of their worst fears.

And that was the hardest part—the feeling that maybe the voice had always been a part of them, buried deep inside, just waiting for the right moment to emerge.

Chapter Three

The weight of Sam's self-doubt had grown so heavy that it felt like they were carrying an invisible boulder on their shoulders, each step becoming more labored than the last. The voice in their head—cruel, relentless, unforgiving—no longer sounded like just a passing thought. It had taken root deep within them, suffocating everything else. They couldn't remember the last time they felt truly connected to anything, anyone, or even themselves.

Each day felt like a fight to get through. The morning alarms felt like a battle cry, dragging Sam out of bed only to face a world that seemed increasingly foreign and hostile. They didn't want to face it. They didn't want to face anyone. In fact, the thought of facing another day made their chest tighten with fear and dread.

The voice was always there, always reminding them of their worthlessness, echoing a constant refrain of doubt, "What's the point? You don't belong here. You never will." It was hard to even breathe through the noise, and Sam's thoughts began to spiral out of control, faster and faster, until they no longer knew where their mind ended and the voice began. It felt like they were drowning in a sea of despair, with no way out, no land in sight.

The idea of tomorrow was unbearable. Sam couldn't imagine facing another day of the same pain, the same exhaustion, the same crushing thoughts. The future felt like a dark abyss that stretched on forever, and all Sam wanted to do was disappear into it. To turn off the world. To retreat so far into isolation that nothing could reach them. The isolation, strangely, felt like relief. It was the only place where the noise of the voice didn't feel as loud, where the pressure of the world didn't weigh as heavily on their chest. But even as Sam began to withdraw more and more, they knew that the pull toward isolation was wrong. They knew that shutting off—mentally and emotionally—wasn't the solution. It was just easier. Easier than facing the overwhelming fear that had taken root inside them.

The truth gnawed at them, even as they distanced themselves from everything. This wasn't the person they wanted to be. They didn't want to disappear, to lose themselves in the darkness, but they didn't know how to fight it. They didn't know how to find a way out of this suffocating cloud.

One particular afternoon, Sam found themselves walking alone in the hallway after class, staring blankly at the floor, the weight of everything pressing down on them. They could feel the tears beginning to well up, but they didn't let them fall. Crying felt like giving in to the overwhelming despair. It felt like admitting defeat.

As they walked the hallway, lost in their head, they didn't hear the footsteps coming toward them until it was too late. In their daze, they collided with someone in the hall, nearly knocking them over. The force of the impact sent a stack of books tumbling to the ground with a loud thud.

Sam froze, their heart racing. *Great. Even the simplest things are a mess now.* They quickly bent down to pick up the books, avoiding eye contact, not wanting to be seen, to make any kind of connection. They just wanted to get away.

"Hey," a warm voice said, soft and steady, "It's okay. I'm alright."

Sam looked up, startled, and saw Maggie, a sophomore student she knew from gym class, standing in front of them. She had short, dark hair and kind eyes, and there was something gentle about the way she held herself, like she wasn't phased by the clumsy encounter.

Sam felt a lump in their throat, suddenly overwhelmed. They opened their mouth to speak, but no words came out. The weight of everything—the isolation, the doubt, the pain, the hopelessness—flooded to the surface all at once, and Sam could feel the tears rising faster than they could stop them. They were so embarrassed, so mortified that they had allowed themselves to fall apart in front of a stranger. But it was too much.

They didn't know how to handle it. Didn't know how to pretend everything was okay anymore.

"I—I'm sorry," Sam whispered, their voice cracking as the tears finally spilled over.

Maggie watched them for a moment, then gently placed her hand on Sam's shoulder, her touch grounding, offering a quiet kind of comfort.

"Hey, it's alright," Maggie said softly, her voice warm and steady. "You don't have to apologize for feeling what you're feeling."

Sam's breath hitched, as they tried to regain composure, wiping their eyes quickly. It was the last thing they expected—kindness from a stranger when they felt so small, so insignificant.

"You don't even know me," Sam said, their voice trembling. "Why are you being so nice?"

Maggie gave them a knowing smile, her eyes filled with understanding. "Sometimes, we just need someone to remind us that we're not alone in this."

The words felt like a lifeline being thrown their way. Sam, still overwhelmed, could barely process what had just been said. But it was enough. It was more than enough.

As Maggie helped Sam gather the books, they felt a quiet shift inside. For the first time in so long, they didn't feel completely invisible. It wasn't a miracle, and the darkness didn't disappear in an instant. But in that moment, Sam realized that maybe, just maybe, there was someone out there who understood—someone who could see them beyond their doubts, beyond the voice in their head that tried to tell them they weren't worth the effort.

And Sam's heart began to open, just a little. Maybe this wasn't the end. Maybe it was the beginning of something new—of finding the courage to ask for help. To reach out, even when it felt like the last thing they could do.

Chapter Four

From that chance encounter in the hallway, something shifted in Sam. It wasn't instantaneous, but in the days that followed, they found themselves thinking more about Maggie's words than anything else. Maggie hadn't judged them when they'd broken down in front of her. Instead, she had simply been there, a quiet, grounding presence in a moment when Sam thought they'd be completely alone.

The next day, in gym class, Sam almost didn't notice Maggie standing off to the side near the bleachers until their eyes met. Maggie smiled—soft and unforced—and Sam, a little surprised, waved awkwardly. They were both new to the class, not quite fitting in yet, and the awkwardness between them wasn't unusual. But as the weeks went on, something changed. Sam had always been the one who made friends quickly, always with an outgoing smile and confidence, but now, with the shadow of self-doubt hanging so close, even the simplest interactions felt like challenges. And yet, with Maggie, something felt easy.

Maggie never pushed Sam to talk more than they were ready to. She just showed up—whether it was during free time in gym or at lunch, where they always found a quiet corner to sit and talk. Sam was grateful for that, for Maggie's understanding. It was like she knew when Sam needed space, when to listen, and when to offer her thoughts—never overwhelming, always just enough.

Sam began to realize how much they looked forward to seeing Maggie every day. Gym class, which had once felt like a place where they were just another face in the crowd, became something to look forward to.

Maggie had a way of making it fun—offering encouragement when Sam felt self-conscious about their athletic abilities, cracking jokes, or simply standing beside them when the games got too competitive or loud.

One day, after a particularly grueling set of relay races, Sam found themselves sitting on the bleachers, as they tried to catch their breath. Maggie plopped down beside them, her face flushed from the exertion but grinning widely.

"You did great today," Maggie said, nudging Sam's arm. "You're faster than you give yourself credit for."

Sam felt a warmth spread through them, the compliment unexpected but welcomed. "Thanks," they replied, a shy smile pulling at the corners of their mouth. "I think I'd be faster if I could actually breathe."

Maggie laughed, and Sam couldn't help but join in. They'd forgotten what it was like to laugh without feeling like something was looming over them, but Maggie had a way of making it feel effortless.

As they walked out of gym that day, Maggie asked Sam if she wanted to join her for movie night. Sam raised an eyebrow. "Movie night?"

Maggie shrugged casually, though there was a mischievous glint in her eyes. "You know, we've got to catch up. You bring the snacks, I'll bring the bad movie choices. It'll be fun."

Sam couldn't help but smile. The idea of spending time with a friend like Maggie, doing something as simple as watching movies and chatting, felt normal in the best way.

And so, movie night became a thing. They would binge-watch movies—most of them terrible, but always enjoyable in their own right. It wasn't about the plot or the acting. It was about the company. Sam found themselves talking more, sharing stories about their childhood, their thoughts about the future, and even their fears about the present.

Sometimes, they didn't talk at all. They'd just sit there, the silence comfortable, knowing that neither of them needed to fill it.

Sam had always been used to thinking that they had to fix everything. Fix their moods. Fix their doubts. Fix the way they felt about themselves. But with Maggie, they didn't feel that pressure. Maggie didn't expect Sam to be perfect. Maggie didn't even expect them to be anything other than themselves, whether that meant laughing at a bad joke or sitting quietly, letting the world go by.

During the next few months, friendship between them grew stronger. Sam found themselves looking forward to every moment with Maggie. The friendship was a safe space, a place where they could just be.

One day, after gym, Maggie pulled Sam aside before they both headed off to lunch. "Hey," she said, her tone serious but kind. "I just wanted to remind you that it's okay to not have everything figured out."

Sam blinked, a little caught off guard by the sudden shift in tone. "I don't really know what you mean."

"I mean," Maggie said, her eyes meeting Sam's, "that you don't have to be perfect. You don't have to be okay all the time. And when you're not, that's fine. But you don't have to carry it alone either."

Sam felt a lump form in their throat. No one had ever said that to them, not in that way. It was a reminder that, even in the darkest moments, there was someone who cared.

From that point on, Sam knew they had a real friend in Maggie. A friend who could be trusted to hold space for them without judgment, a friend who understood that sometimes, you didn't have to explain everything, because simply being there for each other was enough. Sam began to believe that they didn't have to face everything alone.

They still had hard days—days when the voice of self-doubt would come creeping back, threatening to take over. But with Maggie by their side, Sam felt like they could handle it. Not because Maggie could fix everything, but because she reminded Sam that they were strong enough to get through it. And that made all the difference.

Chapter Five

It was a quiet afternoon when Sam finally decided to tell Maggie the truth about that day when they first met and about why it meant so much to them. They had been sitting together on the grass outside after lunch, the warmth of the sun still lingering in the autumn air, but there was a heaviness in the space between them, a tension Sam had been feeling for days.

Maggie was flipping through her phone, a comfortable silence stretching between them, when Sam hesitated. Their fingers fidgeted nervously, the words they had been holding onto for weeks threatening to spill out but stuck somewhere in their chest. Sam glanced at Maggie, whose attention was now diverted to a meme on her screen. But Sam didn't feel like laughing now. They needed to talk, needed to say the thing they had been avoiding for so long.

"Maggie," Sam began, their voice trembling just slightly. Maggie didn't look up at first, thinking Sam was just making another random comment about the meme. But Sam's tone caught her attention, and she looked up, concerned.

"Yeah?" Maggie replied, setting the phone down and giving Sam her full attention.

Sam took a breath, the words feeling harder to form the longer they waited. "I... I've been meaning to tell you something. About that day we bumped into each other in the hallway. The day I almost knocked you over."

Maggie's brow furrowed, confusion flickering for a second. "Oh? What about it?"

"I wasn't... okay that day," Sam said, their voice barely above a whisper. "I wasn't just in a rush or having a bad moment. I was... I was falling apart. Completely falling apart. And when I bumped into you, I was so overwhelmed, I couldn't even hold it together."

Maggie's face softened, her expression full of understanding. She didn't speak right away, just letting Sam continue. Sam had already opened up a little, and Maggie knew better than to rush them now.

"I was so lost," Sam went on, their words picking up speed, as though once they started, they couldn't stop. "I'd been struggling with so many things, and I didn't know how to handle it. But that day? That was the day I realized I didn't even want to try anymore. I... I couldn't see a tomorrow. It all felt too heavy. I thought I was... better off just shutting everything out." They paused, a lump forming in their throat. "I had never felt that hopeless before. And I didn't know who to turn to."

Maggie was quiet, letting Sam's confession settle in the space between them. Sam's eyes darted nervously toward the ground, not able to look Maggie in the eye, suddenly self-conscious about the weight of their words.

But Maggie didn't judge. Maggie never judged. Instead, she reached over and gently placed her hand on top of Sam's, a gesture so simple but filled with understanding.

"I had no idea," Maggie said softly, her voice steady but kind. "I'm really glad you told me."

Sam felt a quiet relief wash over them, the sensation of having shared their truth with someone they trusted. It was terrifying to be this vulnerable, but at the same time, it felt like a weight had been lifted, if only a little.

"I just... I didn't know what to do," Sam whispered, finally looking up at Maggie, their eyes teary but sincere. "But when I bumped into you... it wasn't just the accident that stuck with me. It was that you didn't leave. You just stayed. You didn't even question me, you didn't make me feel like I was... wrong for feeling like that."

Maggie gave Sam a soft, knowing smile, squeezing their hand a little tighter. "You don't have to apologize for feeling like that, Sam. It's okay to feel lost sometimes. We all go through hard times. I didn't know how much you were going through, but I'm really glad I was there when you needed someone."

Sam nodded, feeling a mix of gratitude and vulnerability. "I just... I wanted to say thank you. That moment with you... it made me feel like maybe there was a way out of that darkness. It made me feel like I wasn't alone."

Maggie stayed silent for a moment, her expression thoughtful, before she nodded slowly. "I know what it's like to feel like that," she said softly, looking down at their hands. "I've been there. I've felt like I was stuck in a hole and didn't know how to climb out. But it's not the end. It's just... part of the journey, you know?"

Sam blinked, surprised by the depth of Maggie's words. They had never known Maggie to be the type of person to share much about herself, and this moment felt intimate, like they were both stepping into a place of shared understanding.

As they both sat there, the world outside them seemed to quiet, the noise of their thoughts momentarily stilling. It was as if the simple act of sharing this moment was enough to hold them in place, a bond that, though new, felt incredibly strong. The world around them felt distant, almost suspended, as Sam and Maggie stayed where they were, sitting on the grass. Sam's confession still hung in the air, raw and unspoken for so long. Maggie hadn't pulled away, hadn't said anything to make Sam feel small or less than. Instead, Maggie was there—present, patient, and open.

Sam took a deep breath, wiping their eyes with the back of their hand. "Thank you," they said, voice barely audible. "I just—sometimes I wonder if things are ever going to get better. If I'll always feel like this."

Maggie's eyes softened, and she gently pulled her hand back, her gaze meeting Sam's. "I get it," she said quietly. "I've been there. There were days when I felt like I couldn't breathe, like I was drowning in my own thoughts. Days so dark that I would just curl up in a ball and shut everything out. I didn't know what to do or who to turn to. I thought that maybe this was just... how it was always going to be."

Sam's eyes widened slightly, hearing the depth of Maggie's pain. Maggie, always so confident and easy-going, had struggled too. "But... you're so... you're always so upbeat, Maggie. I never knew."

Maggie smiled gently, though it was tinged with a shadow of vulnerability. "I know. That's the funny thing, right? From the outside, it looked like I had everything together. But inside? It felt like I was constantly fighting a battle with myself. I didn't know how to deal with everything in my head. I couldn't turn it off."

Sam leaned forward, hanging on Maggie's every word. "So, how did you... how did you get through it?"

Maggie was quiet for a moment, reflecting. Her expression softened, her eyes becoming distant as though she were recalling something important. "There was this one day," Maggie started, her voice taking on a tone of quiet strength. "I was in a really bad place. I couldn't stop crying, feeling like everything was hopeless. And then... I ended up in the student counseling office, just talking with this peer counselor. I didn't even know what I was expecting. But she said something that completely shifted the way I saw everything."

Sam watched her intently, wondering what this revelation could possibly be.

"She told me," Maggie continued, "that we are not our thoughts." She let that hang in the air for a moment, letting Sam absorb the weight of the words. "At first, I didn't get it. How could I *not* be my thoughts? They were *mine*, right? If they were in my head, that had to mean they were who I was."

Sam nodded slowly, the logic familiar to them, even if it didn't quite make sense.

"But that's the thing," Maggie said, her voice growing more animated, "we *are not* our thoughts. We have thoughts, but we're not what they say about us." She paused for a moment, looking down at her hands as if searching for the right words. "Most of our thoughts are based in ego. The ego is the part of us that gives us a sense of self, a sense of identity. It tells us who we are, what we should be, how we compare to others. And the thing is, the ego is always *at work*—always telling stories based on fragments and half-truths of the past, and worries about the future."

Sam's mind whirled with this new information. "But... I don't get it. You're saying my thoughts aren't real?"

"They're real, but they're not the truth," Maggie explained. "The ego is always *working*—judging, rating and comparing. It makes us feel like we're either better than someone when we're not or never enough, that we're flawed, that we're falling short. It convinces us that we're worthless or that we're unworthy of love or happiness. And that's not who we are. It's just the ego doing its thing."

Sam felt a stirring inside them, a flicker of something they hadn't felt in a long time—hope. "But what do we do with those thoughts? If they're not real, how do we stop believing them?"

"That's the key," Maggie said, her voice steady now, like she had unlocked a secret she was eager to share. "We don't need to stop them.

We just need to *observe* them. We have to become the observer of our thoughts, instead of getting lost in them. When we do that, we start to see them for what they are—just thoughts. They come, and they go. But they don't define us."

Sam's mind raced, a whirlwind of questions and realizations. "So... you mean I don't have to believe everything my brain tells me? I don't have to let it control me?"

"Exactly," Maggie said, a warm smile lighting up her face. "The ego takes us on a wild ride, especially when we're unaware of it. It's like we're sleepwalking through life, letting the ego dictate who we are and how we feel. But when we wake up to it and become aware of it, when we recognize that the thoughts are just... thoughts, we can stop identifying as one with them. We can step back, breathe, and choose something different."

Sam's chest felt lighter, like a weight had been lifted. For the first time in weeks, maybe even months, they felt like there was a way out. "So, I'm not *stuck* with all this?"

"Nope," Maggie said, shaking her head. "You're not stuck. And you're not alone. The first step is learning to separate yourself from the thoughts and realizing you're not the voice in your head. You're the one who's hearing it."

Sam's heart swelled with relief. "I want to learn how to do that. I want to stop feeling like I'm drowning in my own head."

Maggie smiled softly, reaching out and giving Sam's hand a reassuring squeeze. "You can. It takes practice, but it's totally possible. You're not your thoughts, Sam. You never were."

Sam suddenly felt like there was a path forward, like they didn't have to be consumed by the voice inside their head. And as Maggie spoke, Sam began to feel that familiar spark of hope flickering again, like they might just be able to find their way out of the darkness.

Chapter Six

The next day was Friday, and Sam had trouble focusing through most of the morning classes. Their mind kept circling back to what Maggie had shared—about the ego, about the thoughts not being who they are. It felt like a tiny crack in the overwhelming cloud of doubt that had consumed them for so long. They couldn't wait for the end of the day because the weekend was finally on the horizon.

During gym class, Maggie sidled up next to Sam while they were jogging laps around the track. "Hey, so, I was thinking... how about you come over tomorrow? A few people are coming over, and we're going to talk some more about what we've been discussing. You know, the whole... being aware of our thoughts thing. I think it might really help."

Sam's heart fluttered at the idea, the thought of connecting with others who were dealing with the same struggles. "Really? You mean, like... a group of people?"

"Yeah," Maggie replied with a smile. "Marc, Lex, and Austin are coming too. We've been meeting every now and then to talk about this stuff—how we can start to separate from the voice in our heads and understand it all a little better. It's been super helpful, and I thought maybe it'd be nice if you could join us."

Sam hesitated for a moment, unsure but also eager to explore this newfound possibility of healing. They hadn't really talked to anyone about what was going on in their head, not like this. But the thought of being around people who might understand, who might have felt what they were feeling, was almost too good to pass up.

"Okay, yeah," Sam said, their voice a little unsure but filled with the glimmer of hope they hadn't felt in months. "I'd like that. I don't know what to expect, but... yeah, I'd love to come."

"Great! It'll be good for you, I promise," Maggie said. "We're just going to sit around and talk. It's pretty casual, but it's been really eye-opening for all of us."

As the rest of the day passed, Sam's mind wandered, replaying what Maggie had said. A small group of people talking about what they had been through, the struggles of self-doubt and the tools they were learning to manage it... Maybe this was the thing Sam had been missing, the support they didn't know they needed. By the time the bell rang and they left for the day, Sam felt an exciting sense of anticipation.

Saturday afternoon, Sam arrived at Maggie's house a little early. They had been nervous all morning, wondering what the group dynamic would be like. What if they said something stupid? What if they couldn't relate to the others? But when Maggie opened the door with a welcoming smile, those worries seemed to dissolve a little.

"Hey, Sam! Come on in," Maggie said, leading them through the house to the living room. "Everyone's already here."

Sam stepped inside, greeted by the warm scent of freshly baked cookies and the quiet hum of friendly conversation. Marc, Lex, and Austin were already there, each with their own mug in hand, seated comfortably around a coffee table that was scattered with notebooks and journals.

"Hey, Sam!" Marc called out as he stood up from the couch. He had a laid-back energy about him, his smile easy and inviting. "Good to see you. Maggie's told us a little about what's been going on with you. I'm glad you decided to come."

"Thanks," Sam said, feeling a little shy as they made their way to an empty spot on the couch. They nodded at Lex, a quiet girl with short dark hair who was giving them a welcoming smile, and Austin, a taller guy with glasses and a calming energy about him. He was sitting with his hands in his lap, looking around like he was waiting for the right moment to speak.

"Hey," Sam said softly, offering a smile to everyone.

Maggie made her way over and sat next to Sam. "We've been talking a lot about the ego and how it tricks us into thinking we are our thoughts. But it's hard to break free from it, right?" She gave Sam a knowing look. "It feels like the thoughts are just... *you.*"

"Exactly," Marc chimed in. "It took me a while to realize that I wasn't my thoughts. They feel so real, but they don't tell the whole story. That's the first step—just seeing them for what they are."

"Yeah, but it's not easy," Lex added, her voice quiet but firm. "Some days, it feels like the thoughts just take over, and it's hard to tell what's real and what's just the ego trying to drag you down. The ego creates all sorts of stories based on fragments and half truths. Then we end up time travelling to the past and future with regrets and worries, missing out on what's happening right in front of us in the here and now—the present moment!"

Austin nodded, a hint of frustration in his eyes. "I've been there too. It's like the thoughts become all-consuming, like there's no escaping them. And then you start to believe them... start to believe that you're worthless or that nothing's ever going to get better."

"I know that feeling," Sam said quietly, suddenly feeling like they were part of something real. "It's exactly what's been happening to me. I've been... *believing* the voice in my head."

Maggie added, "You're not alone in that. We've all been there. And it's okay to feel like that sometimes. But you don't have to stay stuck in it."

Sam took a deep breath, feeling the weight of their thoughts lift just a little and nodded. They felt like they were exactly where they needed to be, in a room full of people who understood. They hadn't known they needed this, but now that they were here, they could feel something inside them shifting. Sam felt like maybe they weren't so lost after all.

Chapter Seven

S am was sipping on some tea when they set their cup down. "So, I heard you mention the ego... but I still don't completely get it. I mean, how would you define it?"

Maggie leaned forward, resting her elbows on her knees. "Think of the ego as the voice inside your head that's always talking about 'I, me, mine.' It compares, judges, rates everyone—including you—constantly. It used to protect us, making sure we had what we needed. But when it's left unchecked, it puts us on a roller coaster of highs and lows, always chasing approval or comparing ourselves to others."

Marc nodded. "Yeah. It's why one minute I can feel on top of the world, and the next I'm spiraling, convinced I'm not good enough. The ego's not evil, but it's tricky—it loves to define our self-worth by external stuff like how we look, the things we have, do we have the latest greatest phone and how many likes did I get on my post. That's all meaningless in the big scheme, but the ego thrives on comparing how I am to how you are. When we aren't aware of this it can take us to some negative places, or even make us think we're better than others, which is another lie the ego tells us."

Lex sat up excitedly. "Right. It's that part of us that says, 'I should be smarter, more attractive, more successful,' or 'I'll be happier when *this* happens.' But then *it* happens, and the happiness eventually fades. Basically, it separates us from others, making us think we have to compete or prove ourselves. We end up looking for validation outside ourselves instead of finding contentment from within."

Austin tapped his fingers against his knee. "I always thought I had to fight it—like punch it out of my life—but that just made me feel guilty, like there was something wrong with me. After all, it's part of who I am. But now that I know it's a part of me, yet I am separate from it, I don't buy into its *never-ending* commentary."

Sam frowned, twisting their hands in their lap. "So if it's part of me, do I just... let it do its thing?"

Maggie shook her head. "Not exactly. You just want to be aware that it's a part of you, and that you are more than what it says about you and the world around you. Its always giving commentary on the world, making you feel good if you get likes on one of your posts or bad if you don't get enough likes. Its such a subtle thing that's always present. When I'm thinking about my thinking and feeling bad about it, I become aware that I've associated with my ego, the inner-voice, that inner saboteur, and use tools like Possley's Paradigm to get 'unstuck' from associating as one with it. Its about learning to interact with it differently. And once we're aware of it, we can step back and say, 'Thanks for trying to keep me safe, but I'm ok.'"

Sam's eyebrows lifted. "That sounds... easier said than done."

Maggie smiled sympathetically. "Trust me, I get it. One thing that helped me was giving my ego a name—'Little Maggie.' That way, when it flares up, I can recognize it's just a scared or insecure part of me."

Sam tilted her head, intrigued. "Little Maggie?"

Maggie nodded. "Yeah. I picture her as this younger, wounded version of myself. She's the one who panics about whether I'm good enough, who wants to compare me to everyone else, or who craves approval. When that voice gets loud, I remind myself, 'Oh, that's just Little Maggie feeling scared.'"

Sam leaned forward. "So I'm personifying it as 'Little Sam?' Does that really help?"

"It does," Maggie said. "One time, I was in the middle of a really bad anxiety spiral. I visualized hugging Little Maggie in my mind. I basically wrapped her in my arms and said, 'It's okay, you're safe.' And I just started crying. I realized all those judgments and comparisons were coming from a place of fear—a part of me that just wanted love and reassurance. In that moment, a calm came over me and I centered myself with some slow deep breathing and slowly felt better."

Sam's eyes widened. "Wow. That must've been intense."

"It was," Maggie admitted, her voice softer now. "But it was also powerful because I realized the ego wasn't my enemy. It was more like a little kid who got overwhelmed by the world. When I figuratively hug that part of me, I show compassion instead of going to war with myself."

Lex nodded, her gaze warm. "That's actually beautiful. Usually we think we have to crush or conquer our ego. But you're saying we can just welcome it, be aware of it, and move on."

Austin ran a hand over his hair, a thoughtful look crossing his face. "So, if I notice I'm comparing myself—like, 'He's so much better at sports than me'—I can imagine a younger me, kind of freaking out about not measuring up, and say, 'Hey, buddy, it's alright. We're doing our best.' That's what you do?"

Maggie grinned. "Exactly. It sounds kind of silly at first, but it really does shift your perspective. You see that part of yourself as someone who needs kindness, not someone you have to fight."

Sam exhaled, relief flooding their features. "I like that. I've had moments where my thoughts just spiral—telling me I'm not good enough, comparing me to everyone else. Maybe if I view that as, like, a younger Sam freaking out, I could respond with compassion."

"Precisely," Maggie said. "Because the more we fight it, the louder it screams. But if we offer comfort, if we say, 'I see you, I hear you, but I'm okay,' it tends to settle down."

Marc added, "Yeah, and it stops that endless roller coaster. We're not chasing or running; we're just observing. The ego might still try to do its job, but we don't have to ride those ups and downs."

Lex smiled at Sam. "It's a gentler way to see yourself. No more guilt about having negative thoughts—just acceptance that they're coming from a part of you that's scared. You reassure it, and you move on. Feels a whole lot better than beating yourself up."

Sam nodded thoughtfully. "I really want to try personifying my ego as 'Little Sam,' and hug it when it freaks out. Feels weird, but... also kinda freeing."

Austin laughed. "Hey, weird's good if it helps. This might keep us from fueling insecurities or tearing ourselves down."

Maggie beamed at them all. "Exactly. Remember, the ego isn't evil or bad—it's just a piece of us that can get really loud if we don't pay attention. Recognizing it, hearing it out, but not letting it run the show. That's the sweet spot."

Finally, Sam broke the silence. "Thanks, guys. I feel like I can breathe a little easier. Like, I don't have to 'fix' or 'destroy' this part of me. I just... need to be nicer to it."

Maggie nodded, her smile gentle. "Exactly. Show it love, acknowledge its worries, then perform an action like a guided meditation, some slow deep breaths for a few seconds, or go for a walk or run or listen to your favorite song. That voice will always be there, so figuratively turning your head the other way to an action step, even writing a few things you're grateful for or using a positive affirmation can help as well."

Lex raised her glass. "Here's to being kinder to our own Little Selves."

They laughed softly, clinking glasses in a small toast. Each of them, in that moment, silently vowed to treat their own vulnerable egos with compassion. And with that promise shared among friends, they felt a subtle, yet powerful shift—one that would guide them through every comparison and judgment their ego tried to throw their way.

Chapter Eight

As Sam settled into the conversation, the warmth of the group began to feel like a lifeline. Maggie, Marc, Lex, and Austin were all so open about their struggles—and their tools for navigating the chaos in their minds. For the first time in a long while, Sam didn't feel alone.

Maggie leaned forward, resting her elbows on her knees. "I've been in the same place you're in, Sam," she said softly. "There were days when I couldn't get out of my own head. But what really helped me was realizing that my thoughts aren't me. They're just... thoughts. And when I started using the concepts from Possley's Paradigm, I began to understand that I could separate myself from them."

"You mentioned Possley's Paradigm before. What is it exactly?" Sam asked, shifting on the couch.

Maggie leaned in smiling. "It's this free roadmap I found online—like a practical guide to mental health and wellness. It talks about separating yourself from negative thoughts, being more than what your thoughts say about you and the world around you. It teaches you how to live with and accept difficult emotions, and that by taking small action steps, you can stay grounded in present moment. It's not a cure-all, but it helped me realize I'm more than what my mind says when I'm down."

Sam nodded thoughtfully. "So it's basically a set of steps that helps you deal with all the noise in your head?"

"Exactly," Maggie said. "It's simple, but it's helped me a lot—especially on the days where I feel like I'm sinking. Sometimes you just need a framework that reminds you you're not alone and shows you how to keep moving forward."

Marc nodded, adding, "Exactly. I love the simple framework of the paradigm. I used to get so caught up in the storytelling, always looking back at the past, regretting things I did or didn't do, or obsessing about the future. I was never in the present. But once I became aware of the ego, the voice in my head that was trying to pull me into all that, I realized that I could step back and observe it. I could recognize that I wasn't my thoughts—I was the one observing them. And that made a huge difference. When I'm separate from that voice, I'm no longer living in the past or future. I'm in the moment, and that's where I find peace."

Sam's eyes widened slightly, feeling a flicker of recognition. *Could I really do that?* they wondered. *Could I step away from my thoughts instead of being consumed by them?*

Lex, who had been quietly listening, spoke up next. "For me, I need to do some action step to get me unstuck and meditation has been a game-changer. I found a free technique on the website Imperfection Wellness.com that uses a simple mantra. When I get overwhelmed, I close my eyes and just repeat the mantra in my mind. It helps me center myself, calms the noise in my head, and brings me back to the present. It's like I step outside of all the chaos inside my mind and create a space of stillness. The website has free guided meditations too, it's whatever works for you."

Austin added, "I've found that same stillness in acceptance, or radical acceptance as I like to call it, because it gives the word more power. I just sit in acceptance—whether it's a moment of joy, frustration, fear, or uncertainty—and instead of judging it, I accept it for what it is. I don't try to change it or push it away. I just observe and accept. That's where the real power is: in the acceptance of whatever is happening, without attaching meaning to it."

Sam felt something click in their chest as they listened to Austin, Marc, and Lex. This was the kind of peace they had been searching for. They didn't have to fight against their thoughts. They could simply let them exist without letting them define who they were. The thought of just accepting what was happening instead of resisting it felt like a new kind of freedom.

Lex's eyes brightened. "Yeah, I've been using the concepts in Possley's Paradigm for a while now. The thing I love about it is that it doesn't try to ignore the tough stuff, you know? It just gives you a way to handle it without getting lost in it. It's about intention, action, awareness, letting go, and so much more."

Marc smiled, his energy calming as he spoke. "Yeah, and one of the biggest shifts for me was the awareness of the ego. When I realized the ego is always working—telling me stories based on old memories and future fears—I was able to see it for what it was. I could feel when I was being pulled into those old stories, and I'd simply say to myself, *Oh, that's just my ego,* or should I say 'Little Marc.' Once I recognized it, I could make a choice to step away from it."

Austin nodded in agreement. "Same here. When I learned that I don't have to be ruled by my thoughts, that I'm separate from them, it made all the difference. I started recognizing that I could focus on the present moment instead of getting swept up in worry. And that's where the *next right action* comes in. It's about focusing on one small thing you can do, right now, to move forward, instead of letting yourself spiral into overwhelm."

Sam's heart swelled as they listened to the group share how Possley's Paradigm had changed their lives. The idea of *next right action* resonated deeply with them—focusing on one small step, something they could do right now, felt like a concrete way to fight against the overwhelming thoughts that had been choking them.

Maggie smiled warmly. "You see, Sam, we've all been through it. But when we use the paradigm, we're able to shift out of that spiral. Sometimes it's just about sitting in that radical acceptance Marc talked about, letting the feelings come up and releasing them instead of pushing them down, while not trying to change them. Sometimes it's about surrendering, letting go of the need to control everything. And sometimes, we turn to affirmations or gratitude—focusing on what we're thankful for, or reminding ourselves of the truth of who we really are."

Lex nodded. "The affirmations are huge for me. I use the paradigm affirmation every day—*I am beautiful. I am strong. I am worth it. I am enough.* It helps remind me of my True Self, the part of me that is already whole and separate from the egoic voice that's telling me I'm not good enough or that I'll fail."

Marc smiled softly. "Gratitude works wonders, too. It's about remembering that even on the bad days, there are small things we can be thankful for. It doesn't erase the hard stuff, but it shifts the focus to what we can appreciate in the moment."

Austin chimed in. "I've found that by focusing on gratitude and setting intentions for the day, I can clear the fog of doubt. It's about taking the power away from the thoughts and giving it back to myself. I'm not controlled by what's in my head."

Sam's eyes were wide, absorbing everything the group was sharing. The framework of Possley's Paradigm seemed to offer everything they needed to step out of the darkness and into something brighter, something within their own control.

"Thanks," Sam whispered, the words full of quiet gratitude. "I didn't know it could be this simple... to just separate from the thoughts and focus on what's real, what's here in the present."

Maggie added, "It's a simple daily practice, Sam. But it's one that will change your life, just like it's changed ours. You don't have to have it all figured out right now. Just take it one step at a time."

As the conversation continued, Sam felt lighter than they had in months. They didn't feel like they were fighting against themselves. They felt supported, understood, and hopeful for the future.

And with the guidance of the group—and the concepts of Possley's Paradigm—they knew they had everything they needed to move forward.

Chapter Nine

S am sat quietly with the group, reflecting on everything they had heard. The conversations were giving them a sense of clarity they hadn't experienced in ages. As the group talked about the concept of awareness and separating from the ego, a light bulb went off in Sam's mind. "Now I understand that the thoughts I was so consumed by weren't *who* I was—they were simply *thoughts*, passing like a cloud in the sky. But it's not always easy to remember that.

Marc added, "The thing is, the thoughts will always be there," he said, leaning back in his chair. "You can't control them or stop them from coming. But what you can do is choose how to respond to them. When I first realized that, I felt a huge weight lift off my shoulders. I wasn't failing because I had negative or overwhelming thoughts. *I just had to stop identifying with them.*"

Maggie nodded in agreement. "Exactly. And sometimes those thoughts, when we're caught up in them, can take us to some pretty dark places. The ruminations, the 'what ifs'—they're all driven by the ego. When I start spiraling, I've learned to remind myself that those thoughts are temporary. They're not permanent. But that's where a practice like meditation or mindful breathing can help."

Lex spoke up, her voice steady and soothing. "I used to let those ruminations take me down, like a rabbit hole I couldn't escape. But I've learned that when I'm caught up in those thoughts, the most powerful thing I can do is turn to a simple wellness practice to shift my focus. Meditation is one of the tools that works for me. I use my mantra to break the cycle of overthinking, to pull myself back into the present moment. When I do that, I stop identifying with the thoughts, and I just *am*—I'm not what the thoughts are telling me I am. I'm not lost in the past or consumed by worries of the future. I'm here, now."

Sam was absorbing every word. The idea of turning to something concrete, a wellness practice, when the thoughts felt overwhelming, was beginning to feel more like a lifeline than an abstract concept. Maggie, noticing Sam's thoughtful expression, continued.

"Remember, it's not a one-and-done process," Maggie said, a knowing look in her eyes. "It's not like you do one meditation, or practice one affirmation, and boom—everything changes. It's a simple daily practice, a new way of living. The key is consistency. You start to see yourself *separate* from the thoughts and emotions over time. The more you do it, the more you realize that you have control over how you respond. And the more you do it, the more empowered you feel."

Sam's mind started to grasp that this wasn't about *fixing* everything all at once. It wasn't about trying to eliminate the tough thoughts or erase the negative emotions. Instead, it was about learning how to *manage* them—acknowledging that they were there, but not letting them define them. That was the power.

Marc added, "It's also about awareness and non-attachment, and understanding that we don't have to fix everything all at once. We can't control the thoughts, but we can choose how we respond to them and interact with them. Taking it day by day, moment by moment."

Maggie smiled, turning to Sam. "Exactly. And this is where the concept of surrender comes in. Sometimes, when you're so overwhelmed, it's okay to just surrender to the moment. It's about letting go of the need to control everything—letting go of the 'shoulds' and the 'musts.' When you surrender, you open up space for new possibilities. You stop fighting the thoughts and just allow yourself to feel, to be, without judgment.

That's when you're able to let go of the hold those thoughts and false self-beliefs have over you."

Austin added, "Surrender doesn't mean giving up or not caring, though. It means accepting where you are right now, even if it's uncomfortable. And it's in that acceptance that the shift happens. It's like a door opens, and suddenly, the path forward is clear. I sit with the discomfort now, instead of trying to distract myself or numb myself, knowing this feeling will pass. And let me tell you, doing this is so much better than pushing things down, as they only come out to haunt you later. I feel so much better dealing with things head on as they come up and the paradigm helps me do this."

Lex agreed. "It's true. I've found that surrender is also part of the process of self-compassion. I used to judge myself harshly for having negative thoughts or not being 'perfect.' But now, I've learned to be kind to myself. I don't have to be happy or productive every single minute of the day. I can have bad days and still be worthy of love and care. That's a huge shift for me."

Sam sat quietly, absorbing these truths. The idea of surrendering to what was—without resistance—was something they had never considered. But it felt like something they could try. After all, it wasn't about never having dark thoughts again. It was about *how* they dealt with them.

"Okay," Sam said slowly, "I get it. I can't control the thoughts. But I can control how I respond to them. I can separate from them, practice mindfulness, and just accept where I am."

"Exactly," Marc said, his voice filled with warmth. "And that's the empowering part. You're not defined by your thoughts. And you *always* have choices and actions. And when you practice these tools—whether it's mindfulness, surrender, or even affirmations and gratitude—you start to shift the way you respond to life. You get unstuck, and then you stay unstuck."

Austin nodded. "And when you do that, it's not just about getting out of the dark places. It's about *staying* out. It's about creating a new way of living, where you don't have to rely on the negative patterns anymore."

Sam felt a wave of relief wash over them as they understood that getting unstuck wasn't about solving everything in one moment. It was about practicing small shifts every day. The concepts Maggie, Marc, Lex, and Austin were sharing—awareness, surrender, meditation, self-compassion, and the use of Possley's Paradigm as a guide—gave them a roadmap to follow. It wasn't a quick fix, but it was something that felt sustainable, empowering, and real.

"I think I'm ready to try," Sam said, a faint smile tugging at their lips. "To try all of this. To just... live differently. To not be ruled by my thoughts anymore."

Maggie beamed at them. "That's all we can do—try. And with practice, you'll find that it gets easier. It becomes a way of life."

Sam looked around at the group, feeling a deep sense of gratitude. They felt like they had the tools to move forward. They weren't alone in this anymore, and they didn't have to fight against the darkness—they could simply move through it, step by step, with the support of people who understood.

Chapter Ten

S am listened intently as the group continued sharing their thoughts. They were beginning to see how much deeper this work went than just understanding thoughts—they were also learning how to untangle themselves from the attachments that the ego created.

Maggie turned to Sam and said, "The thing with the ego is, it loves to attach our worth to things outside of us. It tells us that if we don't have the right clothes, the right grades, or the right relationship, we're not enough. It constantly compares what I have to what you have. It keeps us stuck in this cycle of needing to *prove* our worth based on external things. But the truth is, my worth isn't tied to any of that. My worth is inherent to me. It's already there, just waiting for me to remember it."

Marc nodded in agreement. "The ego thrives on attachment. It attaches to the idea that we need certain things to feel valuable, like the clothes we wear, how we look, or even whether we're in a relationship or not. But none of that defines us. I learned that when I stopped attaching my worth to external things, I could finally feel whole on my own."

Lex smiled, adding, "For me, it's an ongoing practice. When I start to feel myself attaching my worth to external things, I remind myself of the paradigm affirmation. I say to myself, 'I'm beautiful, I'm strong, I'm worth it, I'm enough.' It brings me back to the truth—that my worth is not based on what I have or don't have. It's who I am, right now, just as I am."

Sam felt a spark of recognition. They had spent so much of the last few months worrying about external validation, about the comparison game. Hearing the affirmation felt like a gentle reminder that worth wasn't something to be earned—it was already within them.

Austin, who had been quietly listening, now spoke up with a thoughtful expression. "It's not just about letting go of attachment to things. It's also about letting go of the need to suppress feelings. I used to try to numb myself when the emotions got too overwhelming. But I realized that wasn't helping me. Instead of shutting everything down, I've learned to lean in. When those uncomfortable feelings come up, I don't try to avoid them or suppress them. I let myself feel them, knowing that they won't last forever. It's uncomfortable, sure. But it's part of the process. I take some intentional slow deep breaths to center myself and I know they'll pass, and that makes all the difference."

Lex nodded in agreement. "It's the same with thoughts, too. Instead of being overwhelmed by them, I like to be the observer. I picture the thoughts like they're clouds passing through the sky or like I'm watching a movie. I try not to get lost in the story the thoughts are telling me. It's not easy, but it creates space. And in that space, I remember I'm separate from the thoughts and emotions. I have them, but they don't define me. That's where I find my True Self, the part of me that is already whole and worthy."

Austin added, "That's exactly it. When I lean in and let the feelings come up, I'm creating space too. It's the same with the ego—it's like taking a step back and saying, 'I'm not this thought. I'm not this emotion.' I have the thought, feeling or emotion, but I am not defined by it in this moment...I'm more than this. It's hard to separate yourself from it, but once you do it, it becomes easier and it's so much more freeing."

Sam took it all in. It felt empowering to know that they didn't have to attach their worth to what they had or didn't have, that the discomfort of emotions and thoughts didn't have to control them. It was okay to feel them, to sit with them, and to understand that they didn't define who they were.

"This is great," Sam said, their voice quieter but stronger. "I think I'm starting to see it. I don't have to fight against the thoughts and emotions. I can just let them come, knowing they'll pass. And I can remind myself that my worth isn't tied to anything outside of me. It's already here."

Lex smiled and nodded. "Exactly. It's in you, Sam. Always has been."

Maggie smiled warmly. "And you're already doing it, Sam. You're learning that you are separate from the ego. And always remember your inherent worth. It's a journey, but you've got everything you need to get there. Just keep going, and remember—this is a practice, not a one-time fix."

Sam nodded slowly, feeling a new sense of clarity. They were beginning to understand that life wasn't about eliminating discomfort or perfecting every moment. It was about practicing presence, choosing to detach from the stories their thoughts told them, and finding peace in simply being who they were, without judgment or comparison.

"I've been so caught up in these thoughts," Sam began, their voice quieter than usual, but there was a new steadiness to it. "I used to think that because these thoughts came from *me*, they must be *me*. That the fear, the doubt, the worry... it was who I was. It's hard to even explain, but I felt like I was just *stuck* in them, like they were the only reality I could see."

They paused for a moment, gathering their thoughts, then continued, "But now, after hearing all of you talk, I'm starting to get it. These thoughts and self-beliefs aren't me. They're just... thoughts and they're based in fear, from the ego that we all have. They come and go, like clouds in the sky or leaves floating downstream. And the crazy thing is, I don't have to identify with them. I don't have to let them control me anymore. It's like I can step back, being the observer, and look at them from a distance, without getting lost in the story they're telling me."

Sam glanced around at the group, feeling a warmth rise in their chest as they realized how much they had grown since that first day they met Maggie. "What really hits me is that I don't have to go through this alone. I have all of you. I have this group—this circle of people who understand. And I have something that I can turn to when I need it. This paradigm... the concepts we've been talking about. They're like a roadmap, something I can follow when I feel lost."

They took a deep breath, the sense of relief growing as they spoke. "It's not going to be easy, I know that. These thoughts will still come up, and sometimes I'll get overwhelmed. But now I know where to turn. I know I can come back to the present moment, and I can remember that I am separate from my thoughts. I'm not defined by them. And I have tools to help me when I get stuck—like leaning into the uncomfortable feelings instead of trying to numb them, or using my affirmation to remind myself of my worth."

A sense of quiet confidence was starting to bloom inside Sam. They had been living in a world of uncertainty and fear, but now, they felt like they had a way forward, and they had a support system in their friends.

"I think I'm starting to feel a little more in control," Sam said, their voice growing stronger as they spoke. "Before, it felt like I was just reacting to everything, letting the thoughts and emotions control me. But now... I feel like I have a choice. Like I can step back, take a breath, and choose how I want to respond."

Marc smiled at them. "Exactly. It's all about awareness. Once you realize you're not your thoughts, you can choose a different path. You don't have to let the ego run the show anymore."

Lex added, "And remember, you don't have to be perfect. It's a practice. Some days will be harder than others, but that's okay. What matters is that you have the tools to get back on track when you need them."

Sam nodded, feeling the weight of their words sink in. "I'm starting to believe that. This isn't about fixing everything all at once. It's about *living* differently. It's about knowing that I can face the challenges, and I don't have to do it alone. I have all of you, and I have the tools to help me find my way."

And as the conversation continued, Sam knew they were beginning to build the foundation for something stronger than self-doubt. Something that, even on the hard days, would be there to help them stay grounded. Something that would remind them: **I am separate from my thoughts and what they say about me and the world around me!**

Maggie smiled as she listened to the group share their personal practices. "One last thing I want to mention that has really helped me is setting an intention and performing the next right action. Instead of falling into old habits like isolating, numbing, or mindlessly scrolling through social media, setting an intention gives me something positive to focus on. It's like a guide that steers me away from the habits that keep me stuck. Once I've set my intention, I just perform the next right action, no matter how small it is. It doesn't have to be perfect, but it's a step forward."

Sam listened intently, starting to feel the impact of these small but powerful shifts. "I see what you mean," they said, their voice thoughtful. "It's like you're choosing to do something that brings you out of that headspace, instead of letting the mind take over."

Maggie nodded, her eyes bright with understanding. "Exactly. It's not about big, dramatic changes. It's about practicing simple actions that align with who you want to be. For me, the intention could be something small, like 'I'm going to stay present right now' or 'I'm going to do something that nourishes my body or my soul.' And then I just do it. And the more I practice it, the easier it gets to stay out of that spiral."

Lex jumped in, nodding her head in agreement. "That's why I practice mindfulness, especially doing things at 'half speed.' It sounds strange, but when I wash my hands or get dressed in the morning, I consciously slow down. I try to do these simple tasks at half speed, and it really makes me focus. It brings me back into the present moment because it forces me to really *think* about what I'm doing. I don't just go through the motions. I stop, I breathe, and I become aware of the sensations of what I'm doing, whether it's the water running over my hands or the feeling of the fabric as I put it on. It might seem small, but it's a way of staying grounded."

Austin grinned as he jumped into the conversation. "I love that, Lex. I totally agree. For me, it's exercise. When I'm feeling overwhelmed or stuck in my thoughts, I'll get outside, go for a run, or if I can't, I'll do 25 jumping jacks right in the middle of whatever I'm doing. It sounds silly, but it works. Not only am I getting rid of the stress, but I'm also counting my jumping jacks. And here's the key—it's impossible for me to be lost in my thoughts while I'm counting. The act of focusing on the number of jumping jacks takes me completely out of my head, if only for a moment. Then I'm present with what I'm doing, and it helps me detach from whatever my mind was spiraling into."

Sam couldn't help but smile at the simplicity of it all. "I never would have thought that something so simple could have such a big impact. Just jumping jacks or washing my hands slower... that sounds so doable."

Austin laughed. "It really is. It's those little moments of action, of shifting our focus away from the thoughts that try to take over, that make all the difference. And that's what I love about this paradigm we're learning. It's not about getting rid of all the negative stuff. It's about understanding it, separating from it, and then making small choices that lead us back to the present. It's the little steps that make a huge difference."

Lex added, "It's like we're all learning to be the observer of our thoughts, instead of getting swept up in them. Whether it's through mindfulness, intention setting, or physical movement, we're learning how to find our True Selves—our inherent worth—no matter what our minds are telling us."

Maggie smiled warmly at Sam, proud of their progress. "And remember, the journey is ongoing. Some days will feel harder than others, but the important thing is that you're practicing, learning, and finding new ways to navigate your thoughts. And when you set an intention, take action, and practice these tools, you create space for your True Self to shine through. It's all about progress, not perfection."

Sam sat back, feeling a sense of peace wash over them. They realized that they didn't have to be defined by their thoughts, fears, or self-doubt. With the support of this group and the tools they were learning, they had the power to choose how they responded, to show up for themselves, and to live a life aligned with their true worth. It was empowering, and in that moment, Sam could feel the possibility of a new beginning.

Chapter Eleven

Sam sat on the plush rug in Maggie's living room, legs tucked under them, eyes fixed on a tiny chip in the coffee table. They could hear Maggie, Marc, Lex, and Austin shifting around, getting comfortable as the late afternoon sun streamed through the blinds. There was a comforting hum in the house—the low buzz of the air conditioner, distant traffic outside, and the occasional laugh from the neighbors' yard. It should have felt peaceful after the discussion they were having, but Sam's heart felt like a clenched fist in their chest.

They swallowed hard. Something was building in their throat, and they knew they couldn't hold it in anymore. Sam had opened up about their struggles with anxiety, about the nagging voice in their head telling them they weren't good enough. But there was one thing Sam hadn't said. One thing they'd been too scared to share.

Finally, Sam cleared their throat. "Guys, there's... there's something I've gotta talk about." Their voice was shaky, no matter how hard they tried to hide it.

Maggie looked up, instantly sensing the weight in Sam's words. "What's up?" she asked gently.

Sam let out a breath. "I'm just... I'm scared to say it out loud. But I think I need to."

A hush fell over the group. Marc scooted a bit closer, arms wrapped around his knees. Lex and Austin exchanged a knowing look; they all recognized that kind of fear in Sam's voice.

Sam clenched and unclenched their hands. "I—I've been in a really dark place, you know that. But there were days... days where I felt like there was no way out. I wondered if..." Their eyes began to sting with tears. "If maybe it'd be better if I just... ended everything."

A lump formed in their throat. Saying it out loud made Sam's stomach twist, but at the same time, it felt like releasing a deep breath they'd been holding forever. Across the room, Maggie's eyes glossed over with concern. Austin rubbed the back of his neck, looking troubled, while Lex pressed her lips together, eyes full of empathy.

Marc reached out and gently squeezed Sam's arm. "I'm so sorry you've felt that way," he said quietly.

Sam nodded, feeling the tears slide down their cheeks. "I didn't want to worry anyone or make a scene. But I was so lost. Every day, I'd wake up feeling like... like I was already defeated. I wasn't sure I'd ever see a future where I wasn't miserable all the time."

A moment of silence settled. The weight of Sam's words filled the air, and for a brief second, nobody spoke. Then Maggie drew in a slow breath, her voice soft but steady. "I'm really glad you told us." She reached for Sam's hand and held it gently. "Because I've been there too."

Sam looked up, tears still clinging to their lashes. "You have?"

Maggie nodded, eyes shining with unshed tears of her own. "Yeah. Freshman year, things got really bad at home. My dad lost his job, my mom was working overtime just to keep us afloat, and I felt like I couldn't keep up in school. I was... I was exhausted. Depressed. I kept thinking, 'What's the point of all this?' I felt like such a burden." She paused, swallowing. "And at my lowest, I thought maybe the world would be better off without me."

A tremor ran through her voice. The memory was still raw. "But then something happened—well, a few things. I had a friend who told me about this teacher she confided in, who helped her reach out to a school counselor. I started talking to the counselor and then eventually saw a therapist. I found out about the 988 crisis line—like, if it ever got too heavy, I could literally pick up the phone and talk to someone, anytime. Twenty-four seven. I didn't do it alone, though. I had to learn that asking for help wasn't a sign of weakness—it was a sign of strength. And that's when I started feeling a tiny bit of hope. Like, maybe this could get better."

The room felt charged with emotion, but also with a kind of tenderness and understanding. Sam squeezed Maggie's hand, tears still lingering but now mixed with relief.

"That's... that's what I need," Sam murmured. "I just can't keep all of this inside anymore."

"You don't have to," Maggie said softly. "None of us do. And Sam—what you're feeling right now, it doesn't have to be forever. You can get help. There are people out there who care. Therapists, counselors, friends, hotlines. You name it."

Lex, who'd been silent, spoke up quietly. "I'm sorry, Sam. I wish I had known you were hurting like that. But I'm so glad you told us. Because, listen: you are never alone. Whenever you feel like you can't hold on... we're here. And, like Maggie said, there are professionals and crisis lines."

Sam wrapped their arms around themself. "I used to think I couldn't possibly say it out loud to anyone. But the minute I did, it was like this massive weight lifted."

Austin joined in. "Sam, I can't imagine not having you around. So you gotta stick with us, alright? If you ever feel like that again, text or call me, day or night. Seriously. I mean it. Or you can call 988. It's free and confidential and such a great resource to have."

Sam felt overwhelmed—by the tears, by the vulnerability, but also by gratitude. "I just... I was so afraid of saying anything. I thought it made me weak."

"Hey," Maggie said firmly, "it takes *courage* to reach out. Let's be clear about that: asking for help is one of the strongest things you can do. Feeling hopeless doesn't mean you *are* hopeless. It just means you need someone to help carry the load. And that's okay."

Marc, still close by, added, "You remember how we talked about being separate from our thoughts? Sometimes those dark thoughts just keep looping in your head, and you start believing them. I've been there too. But when you talk it out, when you share that burden, you start to see that it's not the entire truth. It's just a passing storm."

Maggie nodded. "Exactly. I had to learn that 'This too shall pass.' I used to roll my eyes at that phrase, but it's *so* true. Feelings are temporary. They come and go, even the worst ones. And once I got professional help and found a therapist who understood me, I realized the negative thoughts could quiet down, or at least, I could turn my attention away from them. Add the daily practice of some tools—like the ones we've talked about—and I found myself rising out of that depression. I still have bad days, but that's life, right? The difference is that now I know they won't last forever. I'm not afraid of them anymore."

Sam wiped a tear away, exhaling shakily. "Yeah... I guess I never really believed it could get better. But hearing all of you say it... I dunno, maybe it's not just a cliché."

"It's not," Lex reassured Sam. "You know, every time I feel overwhelmed now, I think of that: *This feeling isn't permanent,* and I remind myself of The Rule of 5's, meaning how will I feel 5 hours from now, 5 days from now, 5 weeks from now, 5 months from now and 5 years from now. When I apply The Rule of 5's, I *know* I am going to get over this feeling at some point, which gives me hope, and I also allow myself to feel the feeling instead of suppressing it and storing it. Sometimes I'll even call the 988 crisis line or text the NAMI helpline if I'm freaking out, just to talk with someone. Then I'll follow up with my therapist or talk to one of you guys and I know I'm not in this alone. It just helps."

Austin tapped the side of his temple. "And it helps to remember that those thoughts—especially the really dark ones—are all wrapped up in our fears, our ego, our sense of identity. But we're more than that. We can separate from it, even if it's tough at first. That's what Maggie means when she talks about leaning on professional help and daily practices. You need a solid plan to break that cycle."

"Right," Maggie said softly. "We don't just magically get better overnight. But over time, when you keep reaching out, keep practicing the tools, keep reminding yourself you're not alone, the darkness starts to fade. It's not perfect, but it's so much better than living in constant despair."

Sam closed their eyes, letting the moment sink in. The room felt heavy and light all at once—heavy with the seriousness of what they'd been discussing, yet light with the relief of having it all out in the open. "I'm gonna try," Sam finally said, voice trembling. "To open up more. And maybe...maybe I should look into talking to a counselor or something."

Maggie squeezed Sam's shoulder. "Absolutely. We'll help you figure it out."

Lex gave a supportive smile. "It's one step at a time!"

"I'm just glad you're here with us," Austin added softly. "Genuinely."

Sam felt a swell of emotion rise, but this time it was gratitude. "Thanks, you guys. For not judging me. For understanding."

Maggie shook her head. "Judge you? No way. We love you, Sam. We've all stumbled in the dark. We'll help each other find the light, okay?"

"Yeah," Sam whispered, voice filled with relief. "Okay."

They sat like that for a long moment, breathing in the quiet reassurance of the room. Outside, a car passed by, its headlights sweeping across the window. Sam could feel their chest loosening, the tightness that had been suffocating them easing just enough to let a little hope sneak in.

Eventually, Marc spoke, breaking the hush. "So, who's up for ordering a pizza? I'm starving."

A few small laughs broke the tension, and Sam found themselves smiling. Smiling felt good. It was a reminder that even after the darkest confession, life could move forward. They could talk about serious things and still laugh together, still find those little moments that said, *Things will be okay.*

As they settled on pizza toppings, Sam caught Maggie's gaze and felt a sense of unspoken understanding pass between them. Yes, there were still going to be hard days, but Sam felt like they weren't facing them alone anymore. They had a support system, they knew where to turn for professional help if they needed it, and maybe—just maybe—they could believe the words Maggie had said all along: **This too shall pass.**

And with that, they carried on, together, a little lighter than before, holding onto hope like a quiet promise that better days would come. They would always come.

Chapter Twelve

As the weeks passed, Sam began to feel a shift within themselves. The heavy cloud of self-doubt that had loomed over their life for so long started to dissipate, slowly but surely. They could still hear the voice of uncertainty, but it no longer had the power it once did. Sam was learning to separate from those thoughts, seeing them for what they were: fleeting, sometimes harsh, but ultimately not a reflection of their true self.

With the support of Maggie, Marc, Lex, and Austin, Sam began to embrace the concepts of Possley's Paradigm, using them whenever they felt overwhelmed. The simple act of setting an intention in the morning gave them a sense of purpose and clarity for the day ahead. They would stop in moments of stress and remind themselves, *I am beautiful. I am strong. I am worth it. I am enough.* These affirmations became a lifeline, a reminder that their worth was not tied to external circumstances or the judgments of others, but inherent in who they were.

On the days when the thoughts crept in—when self-doubt threatened to overwhelm them—Sam would practice mindfulness, like Lex taught them, observing their thoughts from a distance. The metaphor of sitting in the eye of the storm, calm amid the chaos, gave them the space to breathe and refocus. They began to practice leaning into uncomfortable emotions, just like Austin had suggested. Instead of numbing out or running from feelings, they let them come, acknowledging them, and letting them pass. It wasn't always easy, but Sam had learned that the discomfort was temporary, and the freedom that followed was worth it.

The group's friendship continued to grow stronger. Each of them had their own battles, but they found comfort in knowing they didn't have to face them alone. They would meet up after school, often in Maggie's living room, where they would share their struggles, their triumphs, and their dreams. Through these moments of connection, they learned to be vulnerable with each other, to listen with empathy, and to offer support without judgment.

As summer neared, Sam stood on the cusp of a new chapter, feeling a mix of excitement and gratitude. The road ahead wouldn't always be smooth, but they had learned that they were capable of navigating it. The group of friends, once strangers to each other, had become their chosen family. They had supported each other through the darkest moments, and they would continue to support each other as they stepped into the future.

Sam stayed close with Maggie, Marc, Lex, and Austin over the summer. They kept in touch through text messages, weekend meetups, and even video calls when life took them in different directions. No matter how far apart they were physically, the bond they shared remained unbreakable. They would continue to meet, talk, laugh, and lean on one another. Each of them knew that life would bring new challenges, but they also knew they were better equipped to handle them because of the lessons they had learned together.

The concepts of Possley's Paradigm, like awareness, acceptance, be the observer, surrender, gratitude, and affirmations, became more than just concepts. They were a roadmap to follow, way of living, a way of seeing the world and themselves with clarity and compassion. And as they moved forward, Sam knew that they were not defined by their thoughts or the challenges life threw their way. They were defined by their ability to choose who they wanted to be, every single day.

Sam's future was bright. And while there would still be moments of uncertainty, they now knew how to turn to their friends, to the tools they had learned, and to the unwavering belief that, no matter what, they were enough.

When Sam looked back on that pivotal year of high school, they could hardly believe how far they'd come. They still remembered the heavy weight of self-doubt, the relentless voice in their head that once convinced them they were nothing more than their fears and insecurities. But through the support of their friends, and by using the concepts in Possley's Paradigm, Sam had learned to see their thoughts for what they really were—just thoughts, not absolute truths.

Beyond the concepts they'd practiced—mindfulness, awareness of the ego, leaning in, and letting go—Sam realized that the real magic came from the relationships they cultivated. Through shared tears, late-night laughs, and heartfelt conversations, the five friends forged a bond that neither time nor distance could break. They understood each other's struggles in a profound way. They knew when to offer a hug, when to listen quietly, and when to remind each other that this life was a journey, not a sprint to perfection.

Sam now felt a steady current of hope running beneath it all. They had the knowledge that they were not alone. Whenever life threw them a curveball—whether it was school challenges, family pressures, or new forms of self-doubt—they knew there was a solid circle of support and a set of powerful tools waiting for them.

The five friends stepped into the next chapters of their lives and carried this shared wisdom like a precious keepsake. They learned to set intentions every morning, to pause when overwhelmed, and to perform the smallest next right action—whether it was meditation, jumping jacks, or simply being present for a friend in need. They gave each other space to grow, cheered each other on, and reminded one another that the journey was sometimes messy but always worth it, and this feeling lasted all throughout their high school years and beyond.

Over time, they scattered to different colleges, different jobs, and different corners of life. Yet their bond only deepened. Through texts, calls, and spontaneous road trips, they stayed connected, celebrating successes and providing comfort through disappointments. They were each other's sounding boards, confidants, and biggest fans. And every time Sam felt that creeping darkness of doubt slip back into their mind, they recalled the words of Maggie: *"You are separate from your thoughts. You are separate from what your thoughts and self-beliefs say about you and the world around you. And most importantly, you are enough just as you are."*

By the time they reached the milestones of young adulthood—first apartments, new relationships, career changes—each of them had carried forward the foundation they'd built in high school. The introspective journaling, the mindful moments at "half speed," the clarity of setting intentions, the heartfelt affirmations, and the choice to face feelings instead of burying them—all of it continued to shape their lives in subtle, powerful ways.

Looking back, Sam realized that the greatest victory wasn't eradicating self-doubt entirely, but learning to coexist with it—acknowledging its presence without letting it define them. In doing so, Sam had found a quiet yet unwavering confidence that made the future feel bright and open with possibility. The same was true for each friend: Marc found peace in staying present, Lex maintained her practice of mindful observation, Austin brought a playful energy to everything he did, and Maggie continued to guide others with compassion and wisdom.

And so, the five friends, once strangers to each other's pain and insecurities, walked away with a roadmap to navigate the uncertainties of life, a deeper understanding of their inherent worth, and a community of care that transcended any walls or boundaries. Each of them faced the horizon with a heart full of courage, knowing that even when storm clouds gathered, they had the tools—and each other—to guide them home to the truth: **they were not their thoughts, and they were enough exactly as they were in this very present moment.**

For a free daily prompt journal to reinforce the concepts discussed here, visit ImperfectionWellness.com/Journal.

Possley's Paradigm

Introduction

Possley's Paradigm is a roadmap to discovering a more fulfilled, present, and authentic life. Whether you're new to the concept of mindfulness or already exploring ways to bring more awareness into your daily routine, this section is designed to support you. The journey you're about to take involves looking at yourself and the world around you in a whole new way—by recognizing that your thoughts do not define you, and that true peace and contentment are found within.

The Story Behind Possley's Paradigm

This paradigm is a product of my own life's journey—a path shaped by over 20 years of experience in healthcare as a physician assistant, my deep dive into mindfulness practices starting in the early 2000's, and personal struggles that changed my outlook forever. In 2015, I learned Vedic Meditation, a practice that allowed me to quiet my mind and go beyond the constant noise of my thoughts. This life changing experience eventually led me to leave my career in healthcare and focus on helping others discover their True Selves beyond their thoughts. In 2024 I became a Vedic Meditation teacher and decided to combine all of my experience into creating a holistic wellness paradigm that people can apply to their lives wherever they are on their wellness journey.

Possley's Paradigm is a set of ten universal truths. These concepts, when applied to your daily life, help you break free from egoic thoughts and the false beliefs they feed. These concepts are practical tools to help you discover that you are more than what your thoughts say about you and the world around you. With this awareness, you can embark on your wellness journey to finding contentment and fulfillment from within as you live a more authentic life.

Meditation: The Gateway to Deepening Your Understanding of Possley's Paradigm

At the heart of Possley's Paradigm is the practice of meditation. For many people, meditation can seem intimidating or even impossible—especially if you think meditation is about stopping your thoughts. But here's the thing: **you don't need to stop thinking.** In fact, in the two types of meditation I teach, **thoughts are welcome**. The goal isn't to silence the mind, but to create space between you and your thoughts, allowing you to observe them without getting caught up in the stories they tell you. It's this space that helps you realize that you are more than what your thoughts say about you and the world around you!

Through Imperfection Wellness, I offer both free and paid meditation training to help you integrate this practice into your life. Additionally, on my website, I offer free guided meditations which are designed for people with thoughts—because we all have them! The beauty of this practice is that it allows you to live more fully in the present moment without being held back by egoic thinking. In addition to meditation, I also offer free online resources that complement Possley's Paradigm. These tools can support your personal growth and help you break free from the thought patterns that limit your potential. Everything you need is available at ImperfectionWellness.com, where you can explore free content or sign up for a deeper, more personalized meditation training program.

Possley's Paradigm: A Roadmap to Inner Peace

I like to use the paradigm as my personal roadmap to wellness and you can download your free copy at Imperfection Wellness. I have it printed out to reference when I feel overwhelmed and don't know what to do. I reference it when I become aware that I am identified as one with my thoughts and false self beliefs. These ten transformative concepts that makeup Possley's Paradigm help me out of those overwhelming situations when I don't know where to turn or what to do next.

As you explore each one, you'll begin to see how awareness, acceptance, and other core principles can help you move through life with more clarity and ease. Remember, this is your journey—it's okay to take it at your own pace and interpret these concepts in a way that fits your unique wellness path.

By practicing these universal truths, you can detach from egoic thoughts, uncover your true self, and live your life more fully in the present moment. This paradigm offers a pathway to inner peace and fulfillment, encouraging a life less burdened by negative thinking and more enriched by self-awareness and acceptance.

And if you'd like to take it further, you can listen to "The Imperfection Wellness Podcast," wherever you stream your favorite podcasts, to go into greater detail on the ten concepts of Possley's Paradigm as well as other wellness topics.

With gratitude,
Scott

The Nine Pillars of Possley's Paradigm

Awareness: I am aware that I have thousands of thoughts each day and this is normal. I am aware that I am more than what these thoughts say about me and the world around me. I am aware that I am separate from these thoughts and that they are not based in truth. They are fragments, half-truths and stories from the past and future. I am aware that when I am identified as one with the thoughts, I am out of present moment living and it is unlikely that I feel happy or fulfilled as our egoic thoughts always want more.

Attachment: Ego creates attachment to people, places, things, ideas, opinions, thoughts, and self-beliefs. When attached, I can become paralyzed at the thought of not having them because my self-worth becomes tied to these attachments. I become aware that I am more than my egoic attachments. Releasing our egoic attachments doesn't mean I can't enjoy these items, ideas, and opinions. It simply means I am not defined by them. I know I am more than my attachments. I can relinquish, surrender and let go of the emotional attachments I have.

Acceptance: I fully accept everything in my life exactly as it is, the good and the bad, knowing that the past is over, and the future is an unknown. I accept that I am the sum total of all of my choices, and I know I always have a choice, as tough as that choice may be. I sit in present moment, fully acccpting everything exactly as it currently is, was, or will be. I know I am where I am because of my choices, and my choices today influence tomorrow. And I am aware that there are other variables outside of my control influencing my tomorrow, and that sitting in acceptance doesn't mean I don't work towards goals for tomorrow.

Be the Observer (of our thoughts and self-beliefs): I have thoughts like everyone else. As I am separate from my thoughts, I choose to be the observer. My thoughts are separate from me and go by like I am watching a movie, a parade or as passing clouds in the sky. I am the observer of all my thoughts as they go by, saying to myself, "I am separate from my thoughts. I am more than what my thoughts say about me and the world around me."

Surrender: When a situation, thought or idea is too much for me to handle, I put my hands out and surrender to something outside of and greater than me: God, Nature, The Universe, Consciousness, etc. I drop the oars and become the water. I surrender control knowing "this" is bigger than me & will work itself out. Surrender doesn't mean I don't care—it means I trust that the answer is already there or will reveal itself in time once I let go of trying to control every variable. It acknowledges that I may not currently see the solution, but by releasing my grip, I create space for clarity, growth, and guidance to emerge naturally.

Lean-in & Let Go: When I feel an uncomfortable thought, feeling, or emotion come over me, I sit and get centered with my feet firmly planted on the ground instead of pushing it back down. I lean in and feel what is coming up and take slow deep breaths for 3-5 minutes as the energy around this sensation is released and slowly dissolves. The goal is to breathe through the sensation, refraining from numbing, avoiding, distracting, repressing, or suppressing the feeling or emotion. I let it come up and sit in the discomfort. I let go of the judgments, ratings, and comparisons of the ego. I let go of attachment with the thought, I let go of association with the thought. I let go of the idea that the thought defines me. I let go each and every time the thought comes up that tells me I am less than or better than someone else.

Forgiveness: When I forgive, it doesn't mean what happened wasn't wrong or make what happened ok. I forgive for me, if and when I want to, on my terms, when I am ready to, so I can heal and be free of the emotional burden I am carrying. I don't have to forget, and I likely won't, but I forgive and move on for my sake, on my timeline. Forgiveness is about me and also about lessening my emotional connection with a situation that is no longer serving my greater good. It's an individualized personal decision and I am the only one who can decide if and when I am ready to forgive. And if I can't forgive, I show myself self-compassion and let myself off the hook as forgiveness is a journey.

Affirmations & Gratitude: Move into an abundance mindset with affirmations & gratitude. Affirmations & Gratitude are written and said daily to reframe our thinking and shift our mindset from lack and scarcity to one of plenty and abundance. The paradigm affirmation is, "I am beautiful. I am strong. I am worth it. I am enough!" And if you aren't sure what to be grateful for, be grateful for your senses, that you can smell a flower or taste your favorite meal, hear your favorite song or read your favorite book. While you are always encouraged to feel what you are feeling at any given moment, knowing "this too shall pass," Affirmations & Gratitude help take the edge off of a bad day so you don't go into a negative spiral.

Action: When you are associated with thought and are stuck emotionally, or physically can't get off the couch, set a clear intention and act mindfully. Meditate, do 25 jumping jacks, go for a walk, mindfully wash your hands, any of which can cause an action chain reaction! Get unstuck from ruminating thoughts and overwhelming feelings or emotions by performing next right action. In such anxious or depressed states, one can feel physically and emotionally locked down. Take action, any action! Launch into an activity for you which creates space and separation from your egoic ruminating thoughts!

Using the Paradigm

I'm often asked, "How can I apply the paradigm to my life?" To me, the answer is simple—I apply it to every aspect of my life.

I used to be an over-thinker, and I've struggled with ruminating thoughts, but now, I interact differently with my thoughts and self-beliefs. This paradigm has been a game changer for me because I use it daily. At first, this might seem like extra work, but as you begin to implement it, you realize you're getting your life back. You're learning to live more authentically and you can't put a price on that. It's worth the investment.

You start to interact with your false beliefs about yourself and engage with your thoughts in a new way. They no longer control you. Instead, you live with greater authenticity, fulfillment, and a deep sense of contentment and self-worth from within.

With that in mind, here's a list of **real-world situations** where the paradigm can help:

Letting go of anger – Releasing resentment and recognizing that holding onto anger only prolongs your suffering.

Accepting where you are in life as the sum total of choices – Shifting from regret to empowerment by embracing past decisions as part of personal growth.

Breaking free from the need for constant busyness – Recognizing that nonstop activity is often a form of avoidance while learning to be present.

Releasing attachment to external validation – Letting go of the need for approval from others to find your self-worth, instead, finding your self-worth from within.

Overcoming imposter syndrome – Recognizing self-doubt as a thought pattern, not a reflection of reality, and stepping into confidence.

Letting go of the need to be right – Choosing peace over ego-driven arguments and learning to accept differing perspectives.

Finding fulfillment beyond material possessions and societal status – Detaching self-worth from achievements and external markers of success.

Shifting from people-pleasing to authentic self-expression – Learning to say no, set boundaries, and prioritize personal needs without guilt.

Breaking free from perfectionism – Accepting mistakes and imperfections as part of growth rather than a source of shame.

Recognizing when the ego is seeking drama or conflict – Becoming aware of patterns that create unnecessary stress or chaos and choosing a different response.

Detaching from old, false identity labels – Releasing past definitions of self that no longer serve personal growth.

Navigating loneliness without seeking external distractions – Learning to sit with solitude and find contentment within.

Moving from resistance to acceptance in difficult life situations – Letting go of control and embracing what is, rather than what should be.

Releasing the grip of guilt and shame – Understanding that past mistakes do not define self-worth while choosing self-compassion.

Breaking the habit of negative self-talk – Shifting internal dialogue to be more supportive and kind.

Trusting intuition over fear-based decision-making – Learning to follow inner nudges instead of overanalyzing every choice.

Shifting from hyper-productivity to present-moment awareness – Finding balance between ambition and the ability to be fully present.

Recognizing the ego's comparison trap – Letting go of self-judgment based on how others appear to be doing.

Breaking cycles of avoidance and facing discomfort with awareness – Addressing difficult emotions rather than numbing or distracting from them.

Healing from past relationships without attaching to the story of hurt – Moving forward without allowing past wounds to shape self-identity.

Detaching from the belief that happiness comes from the next achievement – Realizing that fulfillment is found in the present, not in future accomplishments.

Recognizing the difference between true needs and ego-driven wants – Understanding what genuinely supports well-being versus what is an illusion of fulfillment.

Understanding that emotions are temporary and not self-defining – Observing emotions without attaching identity to them.

Stopping drinking as a numbing or coping behavior – Breaking free from alcohol dependence and finding clarity, peace, and self-trust in the present moment.

Calming the chaos and sitting with self and thoughts – Learning to embrace stillness instead of seeking constant distraction.

Stopping mindless scrolling – Becoming aware of unconscious habits and reclaiming time and attention.

Stopping ruminating thoughts – Recognizing repetitive negative thinking and shifting to a more present-focused mindset.

Lessening anxiety – Separating from anxious thoughts and cultivating inner calm.

Changing the stories we tell ourselves about others and ourselves – Reframing limiting beliefs and shifting perspectives to foster growth.

Addressing self-doubt – Recognizing insecurity as a thought pattern, not a truth, and stepping into confidence.

Following charm/nudges – Trusting intuition and embracing life's natural flow instead of forcing outcomes with the realization that ***Insistence Equals Resistance***.

Letting go – Releasing attachments to control, expectations, and past experiences.

Surrendering and lessening control – Accepting what is and finding peace in the unknown.

Most importantly, ***learning to love yourself*** – Becoming aware that you are more than what your thoughts say about you and the world around you, accepting who you are, what you are, and where you are, while sitting in the discomfort, knowing this too shall pass. As you surrender, forgive yourself and others, and stop letting attachments define your self-worth. Become the observer of your thoughts and beliefs, letting go of stored emotions and false stories. Find an affirmation that works for you, ground yourself in gratitude, set an intention, and perform the next right action.

Visit ImperfectionWellness.com to learn more about Possley's Paradigm.

Additional Resources for Your Wellness Journey

Always know that asking for help is a sign of strength! Taking the first step to seek support is not a sign of weakness, but a courageous act of self-love. No matter where you are on your journey, these resources are here to support, guide, and empower you. This list is in no way exhaustive, but a list of resources I have used myself over the years and I share them with you, knowing there are many more out there available to you.

Imperfection Wellness
Visit **ImperfectionWellness.com** for tools, insights, and practices to help you integrate Possley's Paradigm into your daily life. Explore articles, guided meditations, and resources designed to deepen your connection with the True Self and find lasting inner contentment.

NAMI (National Alliance on Mental Illness) Hotline/Textline
If you or someone you know needs support, the **NAMI Helpline** is available at **800-950-NAMI (6264)** or via text by sending **"HELPLINE"** **to 62640.** This resource offers free, confidential support and information on mental health conditions, treatment options, and more.

988: The National 24/7 Crisis & Suicide Prevention Hotline
Dial **988** for free, anytime, anywhere for immediate support from trained crisis counselors. Whether you're struggling with thoughts of ending your life, emotional distress, or substance use, this lifeline is available 24/7 to provide compassionate assistance.

Psychology Today – Find a Therapist
Finding the right therapist can transform your wellness journey. Visit **Psychology Today** to search for qualified mental health professionals in your area or online, tailored to your needs and preferences.

ZocDoc – Find a Therapist
ZocDoc.com makes it easy to book therapy appointments. Visit to connect with therapists covered by your insurance or offering virtual sessions that fit your schedule.

Why These Resources Matter

Life's challenges are meant to be shared, not faced alone. Reaching out for help when you're feeling overwhelmed, stuck, or in pain is one of the most empowering steps you can take. These resources provide vital support systems, offering professional guidance, community, and hope. Remember, asking for help is not only a sign of strength, but a profound act of self-care. Let these resources guide you as you embrace a more fulfilling and balanced life. **You are not alone. You matter and you are worth it!**

Note: I have no affiliation or personal interest in any of the resources listed here aside from Imperfection Wellness. These are just a few of the many resources available to support your wellness journey. I encourage you to conduct your own search to explore additional free or low-cost options that may suit your needs.

About the author

Scott W. Possley is the founder of Imperfection Wellness, Meditation & Wellness for the *PERFECTLY* Imperfect! He is a wellness visionary dedicated to helping others uncover their inner strength and live more authentically. With over 20 years of experience as a Physician Assistant in some of New York City's top academic medical centers, Scott has combined his extensive medical expertise with a deep passion for mental health and holistic wellness. As a Vedic Meditation teacher, he merges evidence-based practices with ancient wisdom to offer a unique, transformative approach to personal growth.

His work is anchored in the principles of **Possley's Paradigm**, a framework he developed to empower individuals to separate from egoic thought patterns, embrace the present moment, and find fulfillment from within. Through his writing, guided meditations, and public speaking, Scott creates spaces where people can explore what it truly means to live with awareness, gratitude, and intention.

Scott's heartfelt dedication to improving lives extends beyond individual clients to entire communities, emphasizing the importance of balance and connection in today's fast-paced world. He believes that asking for help is a sign of strength and that every step toward wellness—no matter how small—is an act of courage. His work serves as a beacon of hope and resilience, encouraging readers to embrace their imperfections and rediscover the joy of simply being.

Also by the author

a world where we are constantly bombarded by our own negative thoughts and self-judgment, it's easy to lose sight of who we truly are. ur minds race, our egos compare, and we often find ourselves stuck patterns that keep us from experiencing the joy of the present oment.

More Than My Thoughts, you will learn how to separate yourself om the incessant noise of your mind and discover an inner ntentment that's always been within you. You'll embark on a journey self-discovery, shedding layers of attachment and uncovering the ace that comes from living in the now.

hether you're struggling with stress, anxiety, or feelings of not being ough, this book offers a compassionate roadmap to reclaim your life om the grip of negative thoughts, showing you how to find fillment in the present moment. Step into your true self today and gin living a life rooted in authenticity, peace, and freedom.

Imperfection Wellness
Wellness for the PERFECTLY Imperfec

The Imperfection Wellness Weekly Newsletter

Sign up for The Imperfection Wellness Newsletter, where you'll receive weekly insights, tips, and inspiration on everything wellness—from mindfulness and meditation to self-care and mental health.

As a bonus for signing up, you'll get these free wellness resources designed to help you live more mindfully every day:

- The Simple Guide to Wellness
- The Daily Gratitude Journal
- The Daily Meditation Tracker
- The Mindful Breathing Guide
- The Imperfection Wellness Prompt Journal

Stay connected, stay inspired, and take charge of your wellness journey! **Visit ImperfectionWellness.com/newsletter** and sign up today!

ImperfectionWellness.com

ImperfectionWellness.com is your go-to resource for holistic wellness and mindful living. Discover powerful meditation techniques, expert insights from Scott, and tune into The Imperfection Wellness Podcast for everything wellness or The Imperfection Wellness Guided Meditation Podcast for calming, transformative meditations. Start your journey today. Find your inner-peace and fulfillment from within and learn to live more authentically, one day at a time.

ImperfectionWellness.com   @PossleyParadigm   Info@ImperfectionWel